DUDLEY SCHOOLS
LIBRARY SERVICE

KU-386-207

Schools Library and Infomation Services

S00000696212

For my wonderful Mum, with love ~
J.B.
For Isabella, with much love ~
R.B.

696212   SCH
JY BIN

First published in 2008 by Scholastic Children's Books
Euston House, 24 Eversholt Street
London NW1 1DB
a division of Scholastic Ltd
www.scholastic.com
London ~ New York ~ Toronto ~ Sydney ~ Auckland
Mexico City ~ New Delhi ~ Hong Kong

Text copyright © 2008 Janet Bingham
Illustrations copyright © 2008 Rosalind Beardshaw

HB ISBN 978 1407 10497 3
PB ISBN 978 1407 10498 0

All rights reserved
Printed in Singapore

1 3 5 7 9 10 8 6 4 2

The moral rights of Janet Bingham and Rosalind Beardshaw have been asserted.

Papers used by Scholastic Children's Books are made from
wood grown in sustainable forests.

A New Home for Little Fox

Written by
Janet Bingham

Illustrated by
Rosalind Beardshaw

SCHOLASTIC

Little Fox was making music.

"La, la, la!"

he sang.

"Shhh!" said Daddy Fox. "Listen!"
Little Fox stopped singing.

"Tweet-tweet-tweet," sang the tree, sweetly.

"What's that?" asked Little Fox.
"Is the tree making music too?"
"It's Mrs Finch," replied
Daddy Fox. "She's singing
her nest-building song."

"Can I see?" asked Little Fox.

Daddy Fox lifted him up higher and higher
until he could see the little twiggy nest.

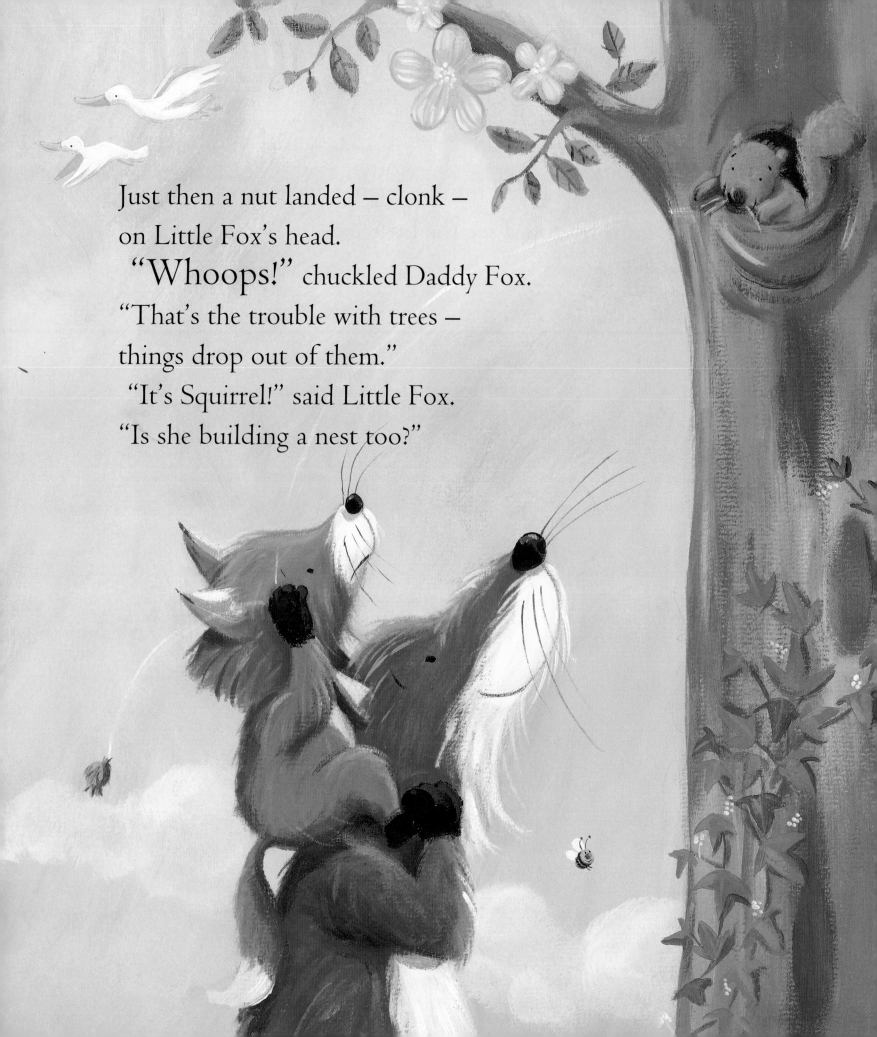

Just then a nut landed – clonk –
on Little Fox's head.
   "Whoops!" chuckled Daddy Fox.
"That's the trouble with trees –
things drop out of them."
   "It's Squirrel!" said Little Fox.
"Is she building a nest too?"

"She's spring-cleaning," said Daddy Fox. "Everyone starts
thinking about their nests and dens in the spring.
They make new ones, or tidy up their old ones…"
"We can make a new home too!" burst out Little Fox.
"Let's build a nest high up in the tree!"

"Trees are too high for us," smiled Daddy Fox.
"They wobble and sway in the wind. We might fall
out of them, like nuts!"

"I don't want to fall like a nut, but it's fun to roll like one," giggled Little Fox.

And away they tumbled...

…straight into a bush.

"Ooof!" groaned Daddy Fox.

"I'm seeing stars."

"They're not stars, they're butterflies!"
laughed Little Fox.

"Let's make our new home here, in
the butterfly-flowers!"

He leaned over to smell the blossom, and yelped,
"Ouch! Prickles!"
Daddy Fox hugged him. "It wouldn't be very
comfortable to live here," he said.

Little Fox scampered ahead.
"Look, Daddy, I've found a mouse's house,"
he whispered. "Perhaps we could live down here."
"We're too big and noisy," Daddy Fox
whispered back. "We'd spoil poor
Mouse's hideaway."

But Little Fox wasn't listening. A dragonfly skimmed past his nose, and he was off…

…chasing and racing over the soft grass. Daddy Fox caught up with him at the stream.

"This is where the fish live," said Daddy Fox. Little Fox dabbled at the water. "I'm glad I don't live in here," he said. "It's wet and cold and runny."

"Like your nose!" teased Daddy Fox.
Little Fox splashed him. "Like **your** nose!"
he giggled, running back up the bank.

All of a sudden, a dome of crumbly earth popped up, with a little pink nose poking out of the top.

"What is it?" asked Little Fox.
"It's Mr Mole," said Daddy Fox.
"He's tidying his tunnels."

Mr Mole's nose disappeared back into the molehill.
"I wouldn't want to live down there," said Little Fox.
"It's **too dark** for me!"
And off he ran to the meadow.

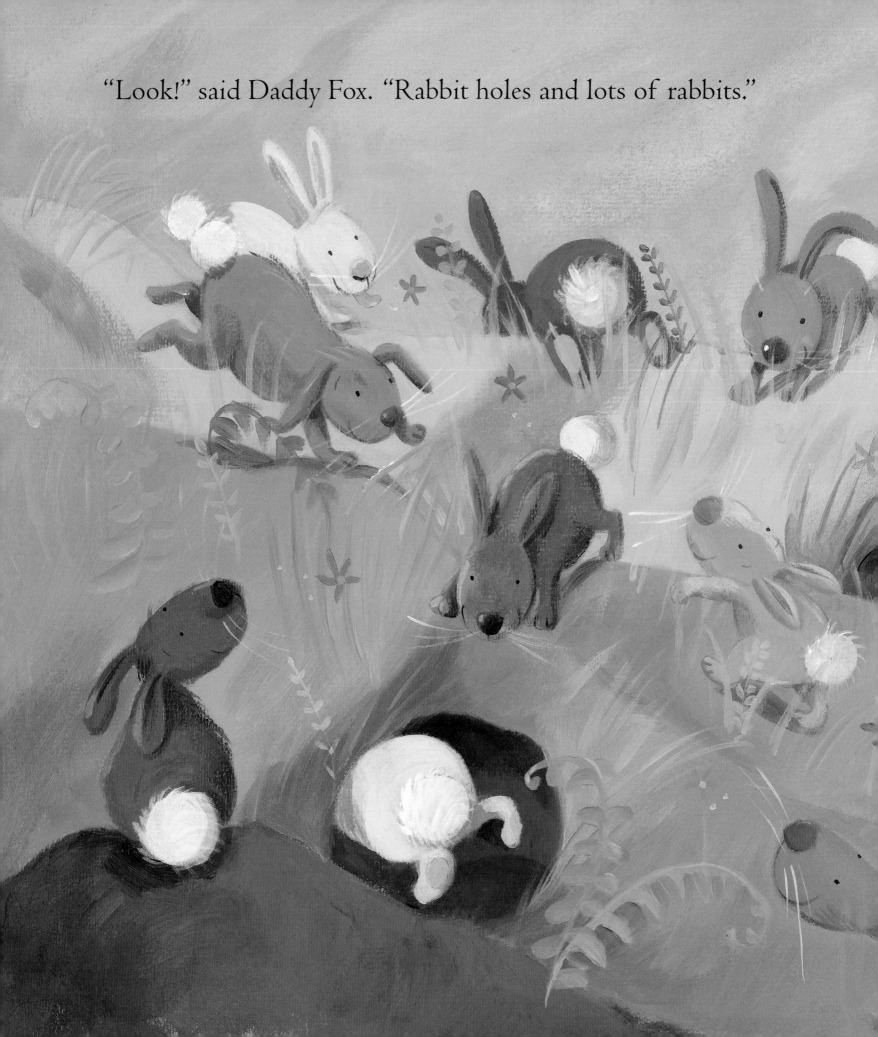

"Look!" said Daddy Fox. "Rabbit holes and lots of rabbits."

"One, two, three…"
counted Little Fox. "I can see ten!"

"It must be very crowded in their house,"
said Daddy Fox. "Come on, it's time to go!"
And they raced away towards home.

Little Fox peered into their den.
"Our home might get crowded too,"
he frowned. "It looks very small."
"That's because you have grown so
big," laughed Daddy Fox. "It's time
for us to move to a new home now."

And that's just what they did.
They dug and dug all afternoon…

…until at last they were finished.

"I'm glad our new home isn't high in a tree or in a prickly bush," said Little Fox, "or in a cold wet stream or a mouse's house or a dark molehill…"

"Or in a busy rabbit warren," smiled Daddy Fox.

That night, Little Fox peeped out
of their newly-dug den.
"This home is just right," he sighed happily.
"Yes," agreed Daddy Fox, hugging him close.

"It's the best home of all…

"...for me and my own Little Fox."